Chanukah Lights Everywhere

MICHAEL J. ROSEN

Chanukah Lights Everywhere

Illustrated by

MELISSA IWAI

VOYAGER BOOKS • HARCOURT, INC.

Orlando   Austin   New York   San Diego   Toronto   London

www.HarcourtBooks.com

First Voyager Books edition 2006

Voyager Books is a trademark of Harcourt, Inc.,
registered in the United States of America and/or other jurisdictions.

The Library of Congress has cataloged the hardcover edition as follows:
Rosen, Michael J., 1954–
Chanukah lights everywhere/written by Michael J. Rosen; illustrated by Melissa Iwai.
p. cm.
Summary: A young boy counts the candles on the family menorah and the lights he sees in the world around him
on each night of Hanukkah. Includes information on the history and significance of the celebration.
[1. Hanukkah—Fiction. 2. Counting. 3. Jews—United States—Fiction.] I. Iwai, Melissa, ill. II. Title.
PZ7.R71868 2001
[E]—dc21   00-8269
ISBN-13: 978-0-15-202447-5 ISBN-10: 0-15-202447-6
ISBN-13: 978-0-15-205675-9 pb ISBN-10: 0-15-205675-0 pb

C E G H F D B

The illustrations in this book were painted in acrylics on board.
The display type was set in Poetica Chancery.
The text type was set in Berling.
Color separations by Colourscan Co. Pte. Ltd., Singapore
Manufactured by South China Printing Company, Ltd., China
Production supervision by Ginger Boyer
Designed by Linda Lockowitz

For my sister, Nancy
—M. J. R.

To my nephews and niece, Sam, Nick, and Emily,
with whom I first lit the candles
—M. I.

On the night before Chanukah, we ready the house for company. My sister helps Dad make up the extra beds, and Mom peels apples for applesauce. I put a new box of candles by the menorah that's waited all year—just like me!—for the Festival of Lights.

On the first night of Chanukah, we say the prayers and light one candle with the tall helper candle. Outside, the skinny moon beams like a proud candle flame against the dark sky

On the second night of Chanukah, two headlights aim right through the window into the living room, where my sister and I spin the dreidel on the floor. Grandpa's here!

On the third night of Chanukah, I switch on the lamps out front
so that my cousins who are coming to visit can find our door—
and suddenly there are three more lights, like in our menorah!

On the fourth night of Chanukah, I find four lights in the kitchen: Mom fries up platters full of latkes, and four flames flicker under the sizzling skillets and the pots steaming on the stove.

On the fifth night of Chanukah, my great-grandma gives me five shiny silver dollars—one for every birthday I've had. When I line them up on my hand, they stretch from my tippy-top fingertip, past my wrist, and up my arm. They sparkle like five more lights in the candles' glow.

On the sixth night of Chanukah, my family takes a walk down the snow-covered streets. And guess what? Six other houses have menorahs gleaming in their windows!

On the seventh night of Chanukah, at my best friend's house, where he celebrates Christmas, a lamp with just one bulb burns in each window— seven altogether, just like in our menorah tonight. Dad says that Chanukah is also about the joy of different religions sharing a street.

On the eighth night of Chanukah, I find all seven stars in the Big Dipper, plus the famous North Star above us, as though God, too, were lighting his own menorah in the sky.

And on the ninth night, which isn't even Chanukah anymore, and the next night after that—and even today—I still see things that remind me of our menorah. And I think about Chanukah and about being Jewish in such a wide world of so many other lights.

A Note about Chanukah Lights

CHANUKAH, also called the Festival of Lights, celebrates a miracle. Long ago, when menorahs burned oil rather than candle wax, a small band of Jews fought King Antiochus's powerful army. The king had ordered the Jews to give up their religion and worship his idols. When they refused, he attempted to conquer them, wrecking their Temple amid the battle.

Amazingly, the Jews triumphed over the king's armies. When they returned at last to their ruined Temple, little lamp oil remained to light their sacred menorah—enough, perhaps, for a day, and yet the oil burned for *eight* days, a sign of a victory that was surely miraculous.

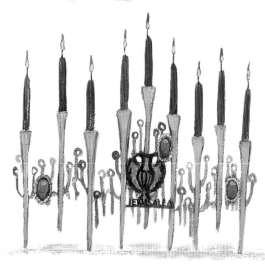

Today our menorahs hold nine candles. The helper candle, called the shammes, lights—from right to left—the other eight candles that each commemorates one day, long ago, that the sacred menorah's oil burned.

Throughout the world, Jews kindle Chanukah lights not only to symbolically rededicate the lamps of the Temple but also to rededicate themselves to their faith with the blessing over the menorah: "Blessed art Thou, Lord our God, King of the Universe, who commanded us to sanctify the Chanukah lights."